DATE DUE

BC-3

JUN – – 1998

L1

Pearl's Marigolds for Grandpa

Pearl's Marigolds for Grandpa

STORY AND PICTURES BY
JANE BRESKIN ZALBEN

SIMON & SCHUSTER
BOOKS FOR YOUNG READERS

To Pam Conrad (Pamel Camel)—
for the memories that remain:
red tulips in the snow,
black beans and soba noodles over the net,
your humor, passion, and inner strength,
your work and poetry—"songs without the music,"
your help in mine.
I will always miss you,
and love you, (benibear)

SIMON & SCHUSTER BOOKS FOR YOUNG READERS
An imprint of Simon & Schuster Children's Publishing Division
1230 Avenue of the Americas, New York, New York 10020
Copyright © 1997 by Jane Breskin Zalben
All rights reserved including the right of reproduction
in whole or in part in any form.
SIMON & SCHUSTER BOOKS FOR YOUNG READERS
is a trademark of Simon & Schuster.
Printed and bound in the United States of America
First Edition
10 9 8 7 6 5 4 3 2 1

Library of Congress Cataloging-in-Publication Data
Zalben, Jane Breskin.
Pearl's marigolds for Grandpa / story and pictures by Jane Breskin Zalben. — 1st ed.   p.   cm.
Summary: A young girl copes with the death of her grandfather by remembering all the things
she loved about him. Includes information about funeral customs of various religions.
ISBN 0-689-80448-2
[1. Death—Fiction. 2. Grandfathers—Fiction. 3. Funeral rites and ceremonies.] I. Title.
PZ7.Z254Pdj 1997
[E]—dc20 96-21596

Book designed by Jane Breskin Zalben.
The text and display type were set in Bembo.
The illustrations were done on opaline parchment
in watercolor with a series seven triple zero brush.
The endpapers are handmade from the bark of a fig tree and pressed marigolds.

In memory of the two grandfathers:
My father, Murry Breskin, who taught me to plant
and called my paintings "love pictures" from very early on,
and my father-in-law, "Saba" Benjamin Zalben,
with love

*W*hen Pearl came home from school, her mother was sitting in the living room. She smiled through her tears and hugged Pearl tight. Tighter than usual.

"What's wrong?" Pearl asked.

"Sweetheart, Grandpa died."

Pearl's mother rocked her in her arms. Pearl didn't mind being treated like a baby. Her mother smelled sweet and felt warm. They sat a long time, until the sun set.

Pearl didn't want to go to the funeral the next day.
She wanted to remember Grandpa playing checkers.
She went to school instead. When Ms. Silver said the
pledge to the flag, Pearl couldn't remember the words.

She forgot what she was supposed to do in art class.
Grandpa had called her paintings "love pictures."
He always hung them on the refrigerator door which
made Pearl feel very special and important inside.

At lunch, she didn't feel like eating or playing tag.
When her friends asked, "What's wrong?"
Pearl said, "My Grandpa died." They hugged Pearl.

After school, she went to her grandparents' house.
All of her relatives were there. Grandma sat on a
low wooden bench while people visited, bringing fruit
baskets and flowers. They ate and talked. And ate.
Uncle Henry smiled and laughed, and it made Pearl mad.
She sat in Grandpa's empty chair. Where was he? It seemed
like a party for Grandpa. And he loved to have parties.

On the chair was Grandpa's favorite hat.
The old felt hat smelled of Grandpa. Like pine needles.
Pearl put it on and went into Grandma and Grandpa's room.
Grandpa's book was on the night table, open to page seventy.
She saw his reading glasses and bedroom slippers.
The slippers were smooth. Pearl slipped her feet inside them
and felt a worn part right where Grandpa's feet had once been.

When everyone left, Mama tucked Pearl in bed.
It began to rain. A gentle *pitter patter*, then
louder and louder on the roof. "Grandpa's cold,"
Pearl cried. "He needs a blanket."
Grandma heard Pearl and came to the room.
Pearl, Mama, and Grandma sat together until
the rain stopped and the moon came out.
Was the same moon shining on Grandpa?

Before Pearl fell asleep, she wondered aloud,
"Who will I play checkers with?
Who will read me stories for as long as I want?
Who will send me marigold seeds this spring?"
Pearl's papa walked into the room. "I will," he said.

A week later, Papa took Pearl to the hardware store—
the store where Grandpa bought Pearl her first shovel.
They got peat moss, potting soil, and marigold seeds.

Pearl planted them. She imagined Grandpa saying,
"Did you water them enough? And feed them?
And thin them into even rows?" Pearl smiled inside
because she saw Grandpa's face in her mind.

When Grandma came to visit, she showed her the
small plants. "Someday, when I'm a grandma,"
Pearl told her, "I'll buy a shovel and giant
orange marigold seeds for my grandchildren.
After we've planted the seeds, I'll let them
pick the red checkers, and win, and read stories
way past their bedtimes. Just like Grandpa."
Grandma gave Pearl a big wet kiss.
"Grandpa's still alive," she said.
Pearl looked puzzled.
"Through you."

BURIAL AND MOURNING CUSTOMS
FROM AROUND THE WORLD

JUDAISM

In the Jewish custom, the immediate family "sits *shivah*" for seven days. For one week the mourners wear black ripped ribbons (or tear a tiny bit of their clothing) and sit on low stools. Mirrors are covered or turned toward the wall. Makeup is not worn. Men don't shave. Slippers of cloth, felt, or rubber are put on instead of leather shoes. Entertainment stops. This is a time of reflection. According to the *Talmud*, the book of Jewish law, the mourners cannot weep for more than three days or remove themselves from everyday life for more than thirty.

Traditionally, the deceased is buried soon after death in a simple pine coffin; the idea being that one's body returns quickly to the earth. After the funeral, before entering the house of mourning, each person washes their hands, cleansing themselves of death.

During *shivah*, a candle burns day and night in the house of mourning for the entire seven days. This *yahrzeit* candle is also lit every year on the anniversary of death, according to the Jewish calendar. A *minyan* (group of ten Jewish adults) gathers together three times a day in the house of mourning to say *Kaddish*, the prayer for the dead. *Kaddish*, the ancient mourner's prayer, is recited over the next eleven months to honor and remember the dead and ease the pain of the mourner.

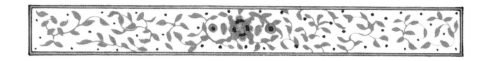

A year later a headstone is placed on the grave. This is referred to as an *unveiling*. People often leave a small stone or pebble on the grave marker to show that they have visited.

The ritual of *shivah* allows one to go through the stages of grief and move toward a path of healing—to understand death is a part of life, and life goes on.

From the *Mahzor*, a special prayer book used during
the memorial service of Yom Kippur, the holiest of holidays:

There is a time for all things under the sun:
A time to be born and a time to die
A time to dance and a time to mourn
A time to seek and a time to lose
A time to forget and a time to remember.
—*Ecclesiastes III*

This day we remember those who enriched our lives
with love and with beauty, with kindness and compassion,
with thoughtfulness and understanding.

ISLAM

Muslims, like the Jewish people, bury the dead as quickly as possible. They too cleanse the body and do not practice cremation (burning the body to ashes). Before burial, the mourners say a series of *takbīrs* (prayers) in the mosque to ensure the happiness of the departed soul. *Du ā* is a silent personal prayer that is said standing, like the *Kaddish*. Some Muslims read from the *Koran*—a sacred book that is considered the foundation of Muslim religion, law, and culture—to honor the relative who died. After these rituals are completed, the deceased is carried through the streets to a mosque, and then to his/her final resting place. As the procession passes, many join in the chanting of the *shahādah*, the Islamic affirmation of faith, and help carry the *bier* (platform on which a corpse or coffin is placed). It is common to bury the corpse in a simple white shroud (all religious Jews do the same), on its side, facing Mecca—the holy city of Islam. Prayers of remembrance are recited for forty days.

BUDDHISM

Buddhists believe in the continuing cycle of death and rebirth. *Karma* (fate or destiny) determines how a person will relive their life. Good deeds may lead to rebirth as a wise and wealthy person; bad deeds may lead to a new life of poverty or sickness. To break the cycle, a person has to eliminate attachment to worldly objects, reaching a state of *nirvana*, or peace and happiness.

The *urabon* ceremony is a memorial service held at a temple. With the assistance of a priest, an offering of food and incense is made to Buddha on behalf of the deceased. The ceremony recognizes the importance of eternal life and ensures that the person will be reborn into a better life.

SHINTOISM

An outgrowth of Buddhism is Shintoism, the national state religion of Japan. The ancient Japanese believed the dead lived on as spirits (*reikon*). Beautiful shrines and tombs are built (often near a brook or with trickling water) to honor ancestral spirits. Offerings, such as first fruits of a harvest, are presented to these spirits. Sometimes lanterns are lit and floated down a river, representing departed souls.

HINDUISM

Hindus also believe in *reincarnation*—that the soul passes through many lives before it is freed. The body is covered with a marigold-colored cloth before it is cremated. If possible, three days later the ashes are gathered and tossed into the Ganges—a holy river in India. Hindus from other countries often send the ashes of deceased family members to be spread in this river.

CHRISTIANITY

Christians believe in *resurrection*—that those who put their faith in God and perform good deeds while on earth will live after death in heaven. Death customs vary among the more than 22,000 Christian sects.

Roman Catholics confess their sins to a priest, asking for forgiveness before they pass on. If someone is seriously ill, the family will ask the priest to celebrate the *Anointing of the Sick*. The priest puts a holy oil on the dying person's hands and forehead as an eternal life-giving sign. The sick person also takes *communion*, which is thought to help one live and grow spiritually as a

member of God's kingdom. By eating the wafer and drinking wine, the death of Christ is commemorated.

In Roman Catholicism, the body is often on view in the funeral parlor for one or two days before the funeral itself. This is called a *wake*, which means "to watch the corpse." The concept of the wake is actually based on Talmudic times of ancient Judaism in which the body was "guarded." (Today in the Jewish religion a person called a *shomer* says prayers and does the "watching.") In the Irish wake there is a festive atmosphere to alleviate the grief. At the funeral there is a brief mass during which the priest says prayers and gives a *eulogy*—a short speech about the deceased. *Mass cards* are sent as a charitable donation in the person's name. They are a way of praying for the souls and honoring the dead.

Some Christians simply hold a funeral and then, at a later date, a *memorial service*, where family and friends perform readings or songs and say things in remembrance. Whether to cremate or bury the body is a personal decision for the family to make. Either way, a priest, minister, or pastor may recite:

Earth to earth.
Ashes to ashes.
Dust to dust.

The spirit of the soul was born and returns to the earth.